FRACTURED ERA ARCHIVES

DECODE

AUTUMN KALQUIST

Diapason Publishing

Diapason Publishing
www.AutumnKalquist.com

ISBN-13: 978-0692443705
ISBN-10: 0692443703

Decode / Autumn Kalquist—1st ed.

Printed in the United States of America

For my husband, Juan.

DECODE

A via entered the skywalk that ran from her research building to the children's hospital. Rain pelted the glass, making the city and the Space Needle in the distance waver and melt. She avoided making this walk whenever possible, and today the leaden weight in her chest grew heavier with every step. But Doctor Phan, the Director of Research at Infinitek Children's Hospital in Seattle, had asked her to meet him there, and she needed him on her side, now more than ever.

Avia adjusted her mask with gloved hands, then walked through the sliding doors to the waiting area of the children's wing. A new wave of dizziness washed over her. The brightly colored murals here were at odds with the tightly packed room of a dozen listless, fevered children and their anxious parents. No one braved the hospitals with kids anymore unless the children were near death.

She tried to keep her eyes from the scene, but she locked gazes with one of the parents, a young father with dark circles under his eyes and a small sleeping boy cradled against his chest. The boy looked to be near three. Ben's age. Avia swallowed against the lump in her throat, and the father's eyes lit up with hope. But the hospital's beds were always full, and she wasn't here to offer hope when there was none. Stomach heaving, she averted her eyes and picked up her pace.

Avia walked into the center of the hospital, and the scent of antiseptic burned her throat and made her eyes water. The closer she got to her destination, the more she had to fight the urge to turn and run back to her lab. Doctor Phan stood just outside his office, next to the nurse's station. He strode over when he caught sight of her.

"Doctor Sherman," Phan said, his voice muffled beneath his mask. "I have a few things I'd like to go over with you."

A pair of nurses ran down the hall, and Avia clenched her hands into fists. She had to keep it together. At least while she stood before Doctor Phan.

He pulled a tan medicine bottle from his pocket and handed it to her.

"Is this... ?" Avia peered at the label. *Grimpanazine*. Grimp stole your emotions, dulled your senses... numbed everything. Half the staff in the children's wing were on it just to cope. But she'd avoided mood regulators for a year, and she wasn't about to start on them now.

"Is this why you called me here?" she asked, her voice flat.

"No, no." Doctor Phan rested a gloved hand on Avia's arm, and she nearly flinched at the touch. "That's not why I called you here. But— it's a low dose, and it's helped many others here. Infinitek's been pushing this latest formulation down the chain. No charge for employees to take it."

Avia was glad the doctor couldn't see her expression beneath her mask. The pity in his voice lit a fire in her. But he was only trying to be kind, wasn't he?

"I'll consider taking it," she said, dropping the bottle into her pocket. But she wouldn't.

"Very good. Now—a new patient just came in, and I want you on her case. I'm heading it up, but we need your expertise. Her parents were part of our early gene therapy trials, and she—"

"I'm busy with my own research," Avia interrupted. "Has there been word on my funding application?"

"Ah. I forwarded your petition for more funding, but understand, you've been pushing this theory for three years now and—"

"It's *more* than just a theory. I know we can improve human immunity. My project is the best hope for fixing this," Avia said, sweeping a hand toward the doors lining the hallway. "You said I could have more time. I need more time."

A child burst into tears somewhere down the hall, wailing. A hospital room door slammed. More masked nurses and a doctor ran past, and Avia pressed her back to the wall to let them pass.

"Let's go into my office," Doctor Phan said.

A nurse led a gurney out from two doors down, and Avia's heart pounded as she watched it, unable to rip her gaze away. A small shape rested on the bed beneath a sheet. Motionless. Silent.   They'd   lost another one.

4

She closed her eyes and took deep breaths, and her paper mask grabbed her lips and stuck there, damp. She never should have come to work today. She shouldn't come tomorrow. Three hundred and sixty-four days ago Ben had died. Right there, down the hall in room 314. The pandemic had taken her first-born, her only child, just the way it was taking the rest of the children and the elderly.

"Doctor Sherman? Come—come to my office."

Avia twisted away from Doctor Phan and jogged down the hall, away from the sick and the dying, back to the safety of her lab.

Inside her lab, the sick feeling in Avia's stomach faded, and she started to breathe normally again.

Her lab was small, but all that would change once she got her funding. Her equipment ran along one wall, and a huge holo screen ran across the opposite wall, in front of her desk. After falling asleep at her desk one too many times, she'd had a futon brought in. Her blankets and pillow lay on it in a jumble, evidence that she'd slept here last night. And the night before that.

She tossed the grimp into her desk drawer and sank into her chair. A message blinked at the bottom corner of the holo screen, and Avia knew it had to be from her ex-husband, Grant, bothering her again. He'd made his choice when he left. Not even a year since Ben died, and he was already living with another woman. She attached her holotab to the main computer system to access her research. A 3D infinity symbol twisted through the air before her and the company's motto appeared below it.

Infinitek: For a Better World.

A better world. That's all she wanted. Global warming. Water shortages. Famine. And then the pandemic. That was the way things had gone, like dominoes, sending medicine and average life expectancies back to the dark ages almost instantly. The developed nations had done better than everyone else, but the drug-resistant bacteria—the superbugs—didn't care where you lived. Diseases they'd been able to cure as recently as four years ago had grown dangerous, and new ones had sprung up—like the numerous flu viruses they were battling now, viruses that had jumped from animals to humans.

Another sharp pain gripped her heart, and Avia flared her nostrils and gestured sharply to pull up her Protected Project files. Just seeing them populate the screen soothed her. She tapped the air, and a 3D molecular structure appeared. She twisted her hand to select a new amino acid combination, and the protein model rotated to accept it.

She waited to see if this would be the match. One piece. One final, elusive piece was all she needed to prove to the Infinitek CEOs that her project was their best hope for humanity's survival in this new world.

0% *match.*

A knock sounded on her door, and it slid open. Avia twisted in her seat, irritated. One of Phan's graduate students, Oliver Dalton, stood at the door, and Avia went rigid in her chair.

"Dr. Sherman," he said. "Can I come in?"

"What is it?"

He stepped inside, clutching his holotab, and the door slid closed behind him. Dalton was the youngest grad student in research, a "genius" who had started grad school before he'd turned twenty. According to the rest of the grad students, Dalton, with his broad shoulders and strong jawline, was just a little too underwear-model good-looking for a scientist. But Avia felt on edge every time he was around. There was something dark about him, something his looks couldn't cover up.

"Did Doctor Phan send you over here?" Avia asked.

Dalton raised his hands and gave her a little half-smile. "You got me."

Avia crossed her arms over her chest. "I'm working on something right now. Get one of the other geneticists to help you. Besides, it's almost night shift. Aren't you heading home?"

"Look, Doctor Phan wants you on this," Dalton said. "A girl came in yesterday. Her parents took part in one of the intelligence gene therapy trials. The trials were thought to be a failure, but—"

"There is a *pandemic* happening right now," Avia snapped. "And *I* am working on superimmunity. Tell Doctor Phan he needs to get his priorities straight."

"Phan wants you on this now, caught up on the case before I leave tonight." Dalton sounded annoyed now, his previously friendly tone gone.

"Ah." Avia pursed her lips and considered Dalton. Good looks couldn't make up for a shitty personality, but he'd had managed to buddy up with Phan almost as soon as he'd started working at Infinitek. "Has Phan said anything about funding for my Protected Project?"

Dalton smirked and glanced at her holo screen. "How is your project going?"

"It's going," Avia said. "I'm close. But I need more funding."

"Infinitek has a lot of projects to fund, Avia—"

"Doctor Sherman."

"*Doctor Sherman*, Infinitek has to fund research on new antibiotics, antivirals, immune-boosting drugs—"

"Like the research Doctor Phan is heading up. Like your research."

"Our work will save lives. Even if your *obsession* proves to be possible... even if you can actually manage to make a gene therapy that *works*, it'll be years before children will be born with your gen mod. I think it's clear which project should be cut off."

Dalton's patronizing tone stung, and Avia ground her teeth. That was answer enough. That's how they viewed her. A sad scientist obsessed with an impossible theory. They didn't plan to continue her funding. "I need to get back to work. Tell Doctor Phan he can find someone else to help him."

Dalton hit the button and the door slid open. "I'll let him know. Team players get funded, Avia. Don't be surprised when they shut you down."

The door slid closed behind Dalton, and Avia felt her cheeks heat up. She was a grown woman with several degrees, all more advanced than the ones *Oliver Dalton* had, and he talked to her like she was a child who needed managing. Well, he could go fuck himself.

But she needed funding. She groaned and jumped out of her seat to hurry out of the lab. Dalton was almost to his wing when she caught up with him.

"If the child needs my expertise," Avia said, breathless, "I'll take a look into her case. But I can't stay long."

Dalton gave her a long, measured look. "I'll take you to her, then."

They passed through the sliding glass doors to the East Wing, and Dalton stopped at the front station to scan his shift card.

The station was filled with observation screens, footage being recorded of everything going on in every room of the wing. Stanley, the old man who worked the station during night shift, glanced up and nodded to them both.

"It sure is rainin' out there, in' it?" Stan's voice came out in the thick drawl of the Deep South, and Avia's heart panged. Every time she came over here and talked to him, she was forced to remember the accent she'd worked to drop and the desperate life of poverty she'd fought to escape. And for what? A failed project, a failed marriage, and a child who hadn't made it to age four.

"It sure is, Stanley," Avia said.

Stanley glanced at his screen, then back at Avia, concern in his watery blue eyes. "I hope you're doin' all right today?"

His question was loaded with meaning. It was clear Stanley remembered when Ben had died, when no one else in her building had. "Yes. I'm doing fine."

"I'm here all night, you know, if you get bored or worn out in that lab of yers."

"Thank you," Avia said, her eyes burning.

"This way," Dalton said impatiently and started heading down the hall.

Avia hurried after him. "So what is this case about?"

"Before you and I ever got here... ten years ago," Dalton said, "they gave twelve test couples a gene therapy that was supposed to help boost the IQ of any child they had together. But it didn't work. They gave IQ tests to the parents, and the children were all within range of their parents, as expected, with no gene therapy."

"Yes, I'm aware," Avia said as they turned the corner. "Has something changed?"

"A girl came in yesterday," Dalton said. "Seven years old. She's the only child of a couple in cohort two. She'd followed all the normal childhood milestones, had never shown any sign of heightened intelligence... until a few months ago. She's profoundly gifted."

Avia's heart sped up, thinking of the implications. This child could be proof that gene therapy could actually *work*. "What's the problem, then?"

"Right when her IQ test scores jumped, she began suffering from sensory issues and seizures. Medication controlled both at first, but not anymore. She hates being touched, and the seizures have gotten worse. They were monitoring her remotely, but now they've brought her in. So we can study her." Dalton's voice brightened on the word "study," and Avia found herself inching away from him. She knew that she sometimes lacked tact and empathy when overcome with excitement over a new discovery, but Dalton took it to a whole new level.

"What data have we collected so far?" Avia asked. They reached a room and stopped.

"Her brain activity isn't normal," Dalton said, as he swiped his card across the scanpad. "The sensory issues seems to be linked with the seizures, but we're not sure how. We have people over in Imaging analyzing her scans. If the seizures continue to worsen, this subject will likely die. We must do as many tests as we can before that happens. In case another child from her cohort begins to exhibit similar symptoms, of course."

Dalton pushed open the door and they stepped into a dimly lit room. A one-way mirror filled up the wall, and on the other side of it a little girl sat at a table, shoulders slumped, drawing a picture with crayons. Skinny arms poked out from the child's too-big hospital gown, and she looked like a wild thing, her brown hair matted and tangled, with blue eyes so pale they made her look otherworldly.

Every few moments she appeared to twitch or shiver. Dalton activated his holotab and began searching through it, and Avia stepped closer to the mirror. The child froze, her hand tight around the crayon. She cast a sidelong look at the one-way mirror, and goose bumps popped up on Avia's arms when the child's pale eyes seemed to find Avia's own. After a moment, the girl dropped her gaze back to her paper and continued scribbling, and Avia let out a breath.

"What's her name?"

"Elizabeth Benton," he said. "Follow me. You can observe while I administer the test."

Dalton typed in his code to open the door beside the one-way mirror, and the girl looked up as they entered. Her face was expressionless, and her eyes slid over Dalton to take in Avia.

Avia offered the child a small smile, but the girl twitched away from them both, her eyelids fluttering, and focused on her drawing.

"Elizabeth, I'd like to ask you a few more questions."

"Lizzy," she said, her voice coming out faint. "And I don't want to answer any more questions."

"Just a few more," Dalton said. He pulled out a chair from Lizzy's table and sat down across from her. The girl jumped up, wild-eyed, clearly fearful of Dalton.

"We want to help you," Avia said, using the same voice she'd used on Ben when he'd met strangers and had been afraid. He'd been such a shy, sensitive boy. She sat down beside Dalton and folded her hands before her. "Just a few questions, Lizzy."

Lizzy features softened as she met Avia's gaze, and she slowly lowered herself back into her chair.

"That's right. We just want to help," Dalton said.

The girl's calm expression vanished, and she glared at Dalton.

Dalton smoothed his annoyed expression and activated his holotab. "This will be just as before."

Lizzy flared her nostrils at him and sank deeper into her chair. Dalton pushed the holotab toward her as the first logic problem came up. A 3D object rotated above the holotab in the air between them.

"Look at the 3D object," a pleasant female voice said from the device. "Which of the 3D objects below it fits into the empty slot?"

The girl narrowed her eyes at Dalton, and then used her hand to push the correct object into the slot. The next challenge appeared, this one harder than the last.

"Look at the 3D object—"

Lizzy moved the correct object into place, cutting off the instructor. Dalton gestured, altering something in the program. A new challenge appeared.

"Look at the 3D object. Which of the 3D objects below it fits into the empty slot?"

It took Avia a moment to figure out the answer. Surely, even a profoundly gifted seven-year-old would take several minutes on this one.

Lizzy's eyes brightened, and she moved the correct object into place.

Dalton shot Avia a look, his eyebrows raised, then turned on the next challenge. Avia glanced around the room, which was a mistake, because her eyes found the bin of toys pushed in the corner. Building blocks, a stuffed bear, a chipped train that had no cars attached to it. The train was from one of Ben's favorite TV shows. Her eyes burned, and it grew difficult to swallow past the painful thickness in her throat.

A few days before Ben got sick, he'd run up to her, his cheeks flushed with excitement. "Choo choo! Watch with me, Mama!"

She'd waved him away and told him to go ask Daddy to watch the show—she was too busy. The pandemics had been all over the news, overloading the hospital with new patients, and Avia had been so driven, working on her Protected Project research even on the weekends.

Grant had been the one to cuddle with Ben on the couch that afternoon, watching the cartoon trains on TV as they taught preschoolers lessons on manners and friendship.

A few days later, every child in his supposedly safe Infinitek childcare room had fallen ill with a mutated form of strep, and only two of the children had survived it. Ben hadn't.

She *needed* the Protected Project to happen. If it didn't, what had she wasted her time for? Because what Dalton had said was too close to the truth. Those last moments with Ben... she'd cared more about saving unborn children than spending time with the child she already had.

Avia tried to wipe at her eyes covertly, but belatedly realized that Dalton and Lizzy were both staring at her. Lizzy's hand reached across the table and grabbed Avia's arm. Tears slid down Lizzy's cheeks, but she didn't wipe them away.

Lizzy's lips trembled, and she leaned closer. "Saving them won't bring him back," she whispered. "But you should keep trying to save them anyway."

Avia's mouth opened, but she couldn't find the words to speak.

Lizzy began to twitch, and her eyes rolled back, her entire body going rigid. Then she lurched sideways, shaking. Avia jumped out of her chair and caught Lizzy as she fell.

"She's having a seizure again," Dalton said. "Get her on her side. I'll call the doctors." Dalton ran from the room, and Avia lowered Lizzy to the floor and turned her on her side as she seized.

Avia closed her eyes and hummed a tune against the fear flooding her in waves, unable to look down at the child. She couldn't think straight, didn't understand what had just happened, how the child knew just what to say. So she sat there, waiting, praying Lizzy wouldn't die in her arms. Dalton came back, and as the doctor and nurse entered the room, the seizure ended, and Lizzy's body went slack. But she was still breathing.

"Keep the equipment in here," the doctor said. Avia heard the words as if through a tunnel. The nurses lifted Lizzy from Avia's arms, and Avia stumbled to her feet and made for the door. She didn't look back at the scene, and Dalton wasn't paying attention to her as she slipped away. She'd go back to her lab to where she really belonged. Dive into her work to forget.

Avia leaned back in her chair and looked at the 3D protein model. She gestured, trying a new amino acid combination. It slid into place.

0% match.

Avia buried her face in her hands and stared down at the scratched metal surface of her desk. She was missing something. If she could just figure out the combination, she'd get her funding. Then she and a team of scientists could formulate a new gene therapy for parents. It would genetically modify germ cells so the next generation of children had superimmunity. No more hospitals full of dying children. Like Ben. Like Lizzy. How would they help *her*?

Avia sighed and looked back at her screen. Two dots blinked in the corner: the message from Grant and a missed comm from Dalton. She'd ignored him when he'd tried to reach her earlier. She typed Dalton's comm code into her holo screen. The comm rang, but there was no answer. She glanced at the time.

11:00 *p.m.* Of course there was no answer. Hardly anyone would be on shift at this hour. She'd been trying to push away thoughts of Lizzy, but what the little girl had said...

Saving them won't bring him back. But you should keep trying to save them anyway.

How had Lizzy known to say any of that? Avia needed to find out more about the child. Before she could change her mind, she commed the East Wing. Stanley appeared on her screen.

"Doctor Sherman," Stan drawled. "What can I do ya for?"

"How is the little girl—Elizabeth Benton?" Avia held her breath.

Stan glanced at another screen to his left, presumably the one with Lizzy's room feed on it.

"She's awake."

The heavy feeling in Avia's chest lifted. "What's she doing?"

"She's colorin'. A nurse brought her in food an hour ago. It's still sitting next to her. Hasn't touched it."

"I'd like to come over to see her." The words flew from Avia's mouth, and the surprised look on Stanley's face matched Avia's own roiling emotions.

"It's mighty late. Doctor Phan'll be in tomorrow—"

"I'm on her case now," Avia said, and disconnected her holotab to bring it with her. "I should talk to her while she's up."

Stanley nodded. "Just hit zero at the door, and I'll let ya in."

∞

Stanley led Avia to Lizzy's room and opened the door. "Comm me if you need me to call the doc," he said, pointing to the comm on the wall. "Any sign of a seizure." He walked out, leaving Avia alone with Lizzy.

Lizzy cringed away as Avia approached her, but then she looked up, and recognition dawned on her face. Her expression brightened.

"I'm glad it's you and not him again," she said. Her voice came out raspy, and she reached to take a drink from the plastic cup of water that sat next to her untouched food tray.

"Who do you mean?" Avia said, clutching her holotab to her chest.

"Mr. Dalton," Lizzy said.

Avia took a few small steps closer. "May I sit with you?"

"Yes."

Avia took a seat at the table and laid down her holotab. Lizzy tilted her head to the side, staring down at the translucent screen.

"What is it you don't like about Mr. Dalton?" Avia asked.

"He does things—to rats and animals in cages." Lizzy's face went pale, and she licked her lips. "And me? I'm just like those animals. He wants to cut me open, too."

"Why do you think that?"

"He's hungry. So hungry. But not for food. He's hungry to do to me what he does to them."

Avia's skin prickled. "What do you think he does to them?"

"He likes how it feels when they cry." Lizzy's voice came out in a near-whisper. "He likes it when they try to escape, and he holds them down to hurt them."

Avia's palms went slick, and she twisted them together more tightly. This child was profoundly gifted, and clearly had a vivid imagination. Avia had seen Dalton trying out new drugs on the animals. He hadn't acted like he enjoyed it, but the discomfort she'd felt around him...

Avia instinctively knew that every word Lizzy had said about Dalton was true.

"Well, I can promise you he won't hurt you," Avia said, her voice coming out strong despite how light-headed she suddenly felt. "I won't let him do anything to you."

"But other people will." Lizzy picked the crayon back up and began drawing again, continuing the pattern of geometric shapes she had strung together across the page.

"Earlier—you said something to me," Avia said carefully. "About saving people."

"Yes."

"Why did you say that?"

Lizzy paused, then kept drawing. "I don't know anything."

She doesn't trust me either.

Lizzy looked up. "I trust you. You aren't like him."

A chill coursed through Avia, and her heart pounded faster. The child had responded as if she'd *heard* Avia's unspoken thought. Could that even be possible?

No. It was impossible. But the things this child had said—she shouldn't know *any* of this. And the way she acted... Was it simply the fact that she was profoundly gifted, or could it be something more? Avia's stomach churned, but she had to ask. Even if it sounded insane.

"Lizzy, when you get the answers right on the tests, do you figure them out on your own? Or do you—do you take them from someone else's mind?"

Lizzy dropped the crayon and sank down into her seat, as if she was trying to disappear into the teddy-bear-print hospital gown. She glanced up at the ceiling, and Avia followed her gaze to the camera installed above them. Of course. This was being recorded, and the girl knew it.

"I want to help you," Avia said. "But we can't stop your seizures unless we know what's happening. Help me help you."

"They're watching," Lizzy said.

24

"I'll make sure they never see this." Avia didn't know what she'd do, but she meant every word.

"Can you put me back the way I was?" Lizzy's mouth turned downward, and she looked at Avia, pleading. "I want to be like I used to be. Before this. I want to just be me, without anyone or anything else in my head. Please."

"Tell me exactly what you mean. How does it feel? What do you—"

In one swift movement, Lizzy lunged across the table, one skinny arm reaching out. She froze, her hand hovering above Avia's; then she let her hand fall, and sucked in a sharp breath as her fingertips brushed Avia's skin. She grasped Avia's hand.

Avia forced herself to remain still in her chair, but her heart pounded an uneven rhythm against her ribcage.

"You're so close," Lizzy said.

"Close?"

Lizzy's eyes took on a glazed look, and she seemed to be staring through Avia. "When I touch you, I can see everything. But I won't remember much for very long after."

"What do you mean?"

"It fades away so quickly."

"You see what?"

"Everything. Everything you know, I know. At least for a little while." Lizzy closed her eyes and stayed quiet for a moment. "I see it."

How could a gene therapy for intelligence— a gene therapy that hadn't even been effective— cause *this*? Whatever *this* was.

If the gene therapy Lizzy's parents had been given had worked, she would be the first child to show an effect from one of Infinitek's gene therapy projects. Lizzy was proof they could work.

Avia stared down at the small hand still clutching hers. Smooth, baby-soft skin, slender, small fingers. *So fragile.* The lump in Avia's throat returned.

Lizzy opened her eyes, and they were glistening now. "You had a little boy like me. His name was Ben."

"Yes," Avia said, and her voice broke.

"It wasn't your fault." Lizzy squeezed Avia's hand. Her brow wrinkled, and she squinted like she was concentrating hard on something. "New life can't grow until you make space by clearing the old."

Avia's lips parted and tears sprang into her eyes. "My grandmother used to say that. An old saying in our family."

"I know." For the first time, Lizzy smiled. "You forgot, so I had to remember for you."

A new wave of grief threatened to engulf Avia, and Lizzy snatched her hand away, as if she'd been burned. She took deep gulps of air and cradled her hand to her chest.

"What is it?" Avia stood. "I'll get the nurse—"

Lizzy caught her breath. "You should." Lizzy pulled Avia's holotab across the table and activated it. She gestured, pulling up Avia's data, a look of intense concentration on her face.

Avia reached over to grab the holotab, but Lizzy picked it up and stumbled away, toward the bed. Her entire body was twitching now, and she dropped the holotab.

Avia ran to the door and pushed back into the viewing area. She tapped in the nurse's code and watched Lizzy through the one-way mirror.

Lizzy was crouched over the fallen holotab now, gesturing wildly. The holotab switched off, and Lizzy jerked once, twice, and fell to the side, seizing.

Stanley answered.

"Send the doctor," Avia said, choking on the words. "Lizzy's having another seizure."

Avia switched off the comm and rushed back into the room. She sat on Lizzy's bed, knocking the holotab out of the way, and cradled the child's head in her lap, stroking her tangled hair as she seized.

Time seemed to drag on forever, until the medical staff finally appeared.

"Get out," the doctor said.

Avia got to her feet and backed toward the door, watching them work. The doctor and nurses attached metallic sensors to Lizzy's scalp and hooked her to their machine.

"Worst one yet," the doctor said. "Track the time."

This was a nightmare. The memory Avia had worked hard to forget—the memory of the night when Ben died—resurfaced. The medical staff in the children's wing, working to revive him, his little body not responding. Because he was truly gone, and when they're gone, you can't ever bring them back.

Avia made it out to the dimly lit hallway and walked quickly back toward the station.

Stanley raised a hand as Avia passed. "Is Elizabeth going to be okay?"

Avia's gaze moved to all the screens around Stan, to all the rooms the cameras accessed. All the hours they recorded.

They're watching.

This telepathy, or these empath abilities, or whatever it was Lizzy had... when she used her gift, was that what triggered her seizures? Avia was sure of that now. Intelligence was one thing, but telepathy? Dalton and Phan could *never* be allowed to see what Lizzy could do. Avia had promised her that. They'd want her to use her gift. They'd study her. She'd die here. Just like Ben had.

"I don't know," Avia said, breathless. "They said—they said they want you in Elizabeth's room."

"Me?" Stanley glanced at Lizzy's cam screen, at the flurry of activity happening there.

"Yes, right now," Avia said firmly. "They said something about the camera feed. They asked me to come get you."

Stan looked confused, but he got to his feet and made for the hallway. "Are you coming?"

"No. I have to get back to my lab."

"You can get through the doors by hitting 'ı'," Stan said, and quickened his pace.

Avia waited until Stan turned the corner, then she moved behind the station and stared down at the array. Knobs, buttons, an old-style keyboard. Sweat popped up on her forehead as she searched for a way to access the recordings. She managed to navigate to a menu on the main screen in front of her and searched down the list. *There.* Room numbers.

She glanced at the screens behind her. The doctor and nurse still crowded Lizzy. Stan entered the room, and one of the nurses pushed him back out. Avia caught a glimpse of Lizzy. She was lying down, but her eyes were open, focused on one of the doctors. Alive. The seizure had ended.

Avia's heart twisted, but she forced herself to focus. Stan would be back any minute. Lizzy's room number was in the bottom corner of the vid. *Room 15.*

Breathing hard, Avia turned back to the menu and selected Room 15 from it. Adrenaline surged through her as the video feed popped up on the main screen.

Access Recording.

Avia pulled up the recording and highlighted the past hour. She hit *Delete.* A new message appeared.

This footage can not be recovered. Do you still wish to delete this file?

Avia's finger hovered over the button, and she swallowed. Should she do it? The data—

"Doctor Sherman? What ya doing back there?" Stan was heading toward her, and he didn't look happy.

Avia jabbed her finger at the button.

This footage has been deleted.

She exited the menu, and the main screen reappeared, looking just as it had when she'd found it.

"They didn't want me in that room." Stan stepped into the station, his brow furrowed. "What are you doing back here?"

"I'm sorry," Avia said, stepping around him to get out of the station. "They did say they wanted you. I was just watching the feed for Lizzy's room. I'm going now."

Stan shook his head and sat back down in his seat.

Avia headed for the door, and it slid open before she reached it. She looked back at Stan. He was watching her with narrowed eyes.

"Please," Avia said. "Comm me if Lizzy has another seizure?"

"Will do. Doctor Sherman."

∞

When the door shut behind Avia in her darkened lab, she realized she'd left her holotab in Lizzy's room. Avia pressed her back to the door, not bothering to turn on the lights, and considered whether it was worth going back for.

They'd bring it to her tomorrow. Along with a demand for her resignation, no doubt, when they figured out that she'd deleted the footage. How could she explain that? They'd *know* it was her. Her mind felt fogged from nights of too little sleep, and though she wracked her mind for ideas of how to help Lizzy, none came.

Weariness overcame her, and she started across the room toward her futon, making her way by the low glow her inactive holo screen gave off. She'd get some sleep, then start researching Lizzy's condition. She peered at her screen to check the time.

12:23 *a.m.*

Ben had died at 12:37 a.m. One year ago.

She made it to her futon and sank down into it. She let go, and the heaviness in her chest imploded, making it impossible to breathe. She pushed her face into the pillow, taking haggard breaths, trying to keep   the tears from coming, but the pain pressed into her, threatened to destroy her, to drag her down, suffocate her.

Avia reached beneath her blanket, fumbling in the dark for that scrap of soft cloth—a remnant of the threadbare blankie Ben had carried everywhere. She huddled into the futon, pressing her lips to the cloth. "I should have protected you."

It had been her job to protect Ben, to keep him safe. And she'd failed. The tears came, and she let them. The heaviness intensified, and sobs wracked her body, carrying her away into the never-satisfied darkness, wearing her out until she had nothing left to give.

A car is coming.

Ben's toy train tumbles into the road.

He chases after it, and I reach for him, screaming, but he doesn't stop.

I close my eyes as the car hits him, steel on flesh and bone. I lift my hands to my ears so I don't hear the sound of his body hitting the pavement.

Because I know this a dream, and he dies every time.

Every time.

Avia forced her eyes open and took in the darkness of her lab. She lifted her hand to her eyes to wipe away tears she'd been crying in her sleep. All the nightmares were the same. She'd lost Ben in an infinite number of ways, over and over, every night.

The holo screen still glowed softly from across the room, and she made her way to the light switch by the light of it. 4:00 *a.m.* She should try to sleep, but Ben had died, and Lizzy needed her. She needed to do research. She flipped the switch and sat down at her holo screen. Her holotab was back in the East Wing, but she could still access the main computer here.

Avia pulled up everything the system had on seizures, sensory processing disorders, and the gene therapy Lizzy's parents had received. Then she got to work.

By the time the clock read 8:00 a.m., Avia felt no closer to figuring out what to do about Lizzy. There was nothing in the literature about telepathy, obviously, and Avia's mind felt nearly as foggy as it had before she'd slept. Phan would probably be here soon about the footage Avia had deleted.

Avia grabbed the overnight bag she kept in one of the cabinets and hurried to clean herself up at her lab's sink.

Just as she was dropping her toothbrush back in the bag, the door slid open. Dalton walked in, carrying a holotab, and Phan walked in behind him. Both of them glanced over at her futon, at her tangled pillow and blankets, the bag on the floor before her.

Phan shook his head, his expression downcast, but Dalton's lips formed into a sneer of disgust.

"What did you do last night, Avia?" Dalton said.

Avia shoved her bag under the futon and slowly stood, meeting Dalton's gaze head on. "*Doctor Sherman*," she said, her voice stiff. "I went to see Elizabeth Benton, because she was awake and Doctor Phan assigned me to her case."

Dalton's nostrils flared, and he looked at Phan.

"Doctor Sherman," Phan said. "The front station records security footage of every room in the wing. An hour of it is missing from exactly when you went to see her and she suffered her seizure. It was the worst seizure she's ever had,

35

and now we have no idea what triggered it. But you were there."

Avia shrugged. "How strange. Did you ask Stanley what happened?"

"Yes, actually, we did," Dalton said, satisfaction in his voice. "He says he let you in and claims that a glitch must have deleted the footage."

Bless Stanley. But she wasn't in the clear yet. Avia clenched her hands into fists and her heart pumped faster as Dalton crossed her lab. He stopped at her desk to attach the holotab to her holo screen.

"This is your holotab. You left it in Lizzy's room last night. But I added on some footage for you to watch. You know... we also have security cameras in every hallway."

He brought up the 2D video, grainy from the dim lights of night shift, and she could make herself out, sitting behind the station. In the video she was looking intently at one of the station's many monitors, but the main monitor's screen wasn't visible from the angle of the camera in the hall, so her actions weren't clear.

"I was just watching Lizzy. I was worried for her."

"You're looking at the main system monitor here, not at the monitor showing the footage from Lizzy's room."

Avia turned to Doctor Phan. "What exactly are you accusing me of? You think I would *delete* footage? Stanley told you the system has a glitch."

Phan licked his lips. "No. No, of course I'm not saying that."

Avia released a breath. "So do you want my help with Lizzy or not? I think I can help her."

"We don't have a glitch in our system," Dalton said. "You said—"

"Did you get the brain scan analysis back yet?" Avia asked, cutting Dalton off.

"Doctor Phan," Dalton said. Avia darted a glance at him. His face had gone red, and Avia found herself taking a step away from him.

He likes it when they try to escape, and he holds them down to hurt them.

Doctor Phan shot an irritated look Dalton's way, then folded his arms across his chest. "We got the scans back this morning."

"And?"

"We still don't know what it means. When Elizabeth is working on a problem, or when she exhibits strong emotion, the parts of her brain we expect to light up, don't. Instead, the parts associated with sensory processing light up. They're constantly 'on,' which is why she has a hard time with any sort of touch. And when that section gets very fired up, she has a seizure. She had one, once, during one of the first tests we did."

Dalton interrupted, clearly annoyed, but Avia blocked their voices out. She turned away from them both, thinking, one hand pressed to her forehead. Lizzy was somehow feeling what others felt, hearing or understanding what they thought by using the sensory processing areas of her brain. They'd need to study her to find out how, but... if they could lower her sensitivity to stimuli, lower her sensitivity to what other people were thinking and feeling—perhaps that would bring the seizures to a halt. Avia's hand slid from her forehead. It was only a hunch, but—

"Doctor Sherman," Phan said. "What are you—?"

"Wait." Avia strode over to her desk and pulled the plastic bottle of grimp from her drawer. "This? How does this work?"

"It regulates emotions," Phan said, his brow wrinkling. "It lowers a patient's sensitivity to—"

"Stimuli," Avia finished. "I want you to dose Lizzy with this. I think it could help stop her seizures."

"It won't have an effect," Dalton said. "Lizzy has a sensory processing disorder, not an emotional one."

"Try it, Doctor Phan. Just try it and see how she feels. Then we'll talk about what happened last night. Do you want the child to suffer a seizure that will leave her brain damaged... or worse?"

"What makes you think this will work?"

"It won't," Dalton said.

"I was doing some research last night. I think her brain processes her emotions and thoughts differently than ours... it's not wired the same. Her seizures come on when she becomes overstimulated. Perhaps if we lower her emotional response, we can halt the seizures."

Phan's brow furrowed. "I can see what you're saying, but—all right. The risk is low. We can try one dose on her, just to test how her brain responds."

∞

Avia watched from behind the one-way mirror as nurses wheeled a machine into Lizzy's room. Lizzy looked up, sleepy, from her place on the bed, then shot into sitting position. Her gaze went straight to the mirror and landed on Avia.

Avia shivered. Lizzy could see her, or feel her, through the mirror. Avia yearned to study the girl, but not if it risked her life. She turned to Doctor Phan. "Please, I've established a connection with her. Let me go in."

"No. The nurses and I will handle this."

"She doesn't even have her parents—"

"This is a low risk procedure, and they've approved it. They will be here shortly."

Lizzy screamed something at the nurse who was trying to adhere the round metallic sensors to Lizzy's scalp.

The nurse glanced back at the mirror, and the second nurse hurried out through the door and addressed Doctor Phan.

"Elizabeth is asking for Doctor Sherman."

Dalton made a noise from beside Avia, who lifted her brows at Doctor Phan.

"Fine,   then.   You   come in with me."

40

Avia followed Doctor Phan into Lizzy's room, and Lizzy pushed the nurse away as Avia hurried to her side.

Lizzy grabbed Avia by the arm, and Avia worked hard to calm the mixture of excitement and worry she felt coursing through her. Sudden doubt hit her. What if she was wrong? Telepathy didn't exist.

She focused her mind on one thought. *We're going to try a drug to help you. Hold up one finger if you can understand what I'm thinking."*

Lizzy's eyes widened, and she swallowed visibly. She held up one shaking finger. "Will it hurt?"

Avia stared at Lizzy's finger and took a deep breath to calm her own mind. "No. You have to let the nurses put on the sensors and give you an IV though."

Lizzy settled back in bed, and tears leaked from her eyes as the nurses worked. Every few moments she'd jerk at their touch, but she managed to keep herself fairly still. Avia's arms ached to hold the child, to tell her it would be okay, but touching her would only make the pain worse. How would it feel to feel the emotions of everyone in the room, to hear their thoughts? She hadn't asked Lizzy how it worked, how touching a person helped the connection, but now wasn't the time. Now it was time to try to stop her seizures.

Doctor Phan gave Lizzy the drug, and then they waited, watching the machine that tracked her brain's functioning.

"It's still the same pattern as before. All sensory. Very erratic," Doctor Phan said.

In the bed, Lizzy shut her eyes tight. The small metal circles were buried in her tangle of hair, and crisscrossing wires were attached to the machine at her side, which showed a 3D image of Lizzy's brain. She looked so small, helpless. Avia hugged herself in the chill room and watched. Waited. Maybe her hunch had been a mistake. Why should grimp help the girl regulate other people's emotions? It didn't even make sense. But Avia had made more than one breakthrough in her years in the lab by following her gut instinct.

Lizzy started to seize, and Avia moved to her, but the nurses and Doctor Phan pushed her out of the way. As they reached her bedside, the seizing stopped, and Lizzie's body went limp.

Then she sat up suddenly, dragging all the wires with her. Her eyes were wide again, a look of wonder in them. She reached out her arms toward Avia. "Doctor Sherman," she said. The nurse and Doctor Phan stepped away to make room for Avia.

"The patterns are changing," Doctor Phan said, his voice rising. He stepped closer to the machine, and the nurses crowded around it with him.

Avia went to Lizzy, and the girl grabbed both her hands, her face lighting up.

"I—"

"Shh," Avia whispered. She tilted her head up a bit, toward the ceiling and the camera.

"It's gone," Lizzy said. She looked joyful, like a child should, for the first time since Avia had met her. "I'm just me. It's only me in here," she whispered.

"I can't believe this," Phan said from his place by the machine. "Dalton, get in here."

Lizzy stared around the room in wonder, at each person in turn, and shook her head. "Nothing. Only me."

Avia focused a thought for Lizzy. *Dr. Phan, prancing around, dressed like a clown.*

Lizzy showed no sign she'd "heard" Avia's thought. The medication really was working. Avia's chest expanded, her heart lightening. "Doctor Phan, what's happening?"

"Her brain patterns are starting to normalize. I don't understand how the drug could do this. We'll have to do more testing, keep a close eye on her—"

"But if her patterns stay that way?"

Doctor Phan's brows lifted. "It's too early to say, but... we'll see if it stops the seizures." He looked back at the screen, and he and Dalton launched into a conversation about brain patterns. Not Avia's area of expertise.

She looked back at Lizzy. "I don't know if this will be permanent, but—can you still feel *your* emotions?"

Lizzy beamed. "I feel all mine, and no one else's," she said, keeping her voice low. She took a moment to yawn. "Thank you, Avia."

"You look tired. You should rest. I'll be here." Avia took Lizzy's hand in her own, and Lizzy closed her eyes.

Avia stood there for a while, holding Lizzy's hand, gazing down at her, until Phan came over and rested a hand on her shoulder. "We're going to monitor her for a while. You can get back to your lab. I... we need to talk about your funding later today."

Avia stepped away from Lizzy and met Phan's gaze. She felt dizzy, nauseated. She

44

didn't want to have this conversation. "No need. I already know you're dropping my program."

Phan pressed his lips together and gestured toward Lizzy. "You made a good call today, but—I'm sorry about your project. I'm reassigning you to East Wing. You can move your things tomorrow."

Avia nodded, trying not to let her emotions boil over, trying not to say something she'd regret, trying not to cry. She pushed past Doctor Phan and hurried out the door.

Hearing it confirmed, that her project was being closed down... all the excitement and relief of helping Lizzy vanished, leaving only regret and deep pain behind.

She may have saved a child's life today, but it was the anniversary of the day she'd lost her own. She just wanted to be alone one more time, in the lab she'd be kicked out of tomorrow.

Avia sank down into her desk chair with a heavy heart. Her holotab was where Dalton had left it, attached to her screen. In the corner, the message still blinked. Avia sighed and tapped the air to open it.

Grant appeared, and heat spread in Avia's chest. New furniture was arrayed behind him, things he'd bought when he'd moved on with his life. She hated him for leaving. She hated him for being unable to move forward *with* her. He'd blamed her for her long hours at the lab, said she'd grown distant, but hadn't he said "for better or worse"?

Avia started the video. Grant looked serious, but his eyes were kind, like the Grant she remembered from earlier years. Was he happier now?

"Avia, I know you don't want to talk to me, but I'll be here for you when you're ready. I still want to be friends. I miss... I miss Ben, too. When you're ready to talk, call me. We can meet up. I'll even drive up to Seattle to see you."

He cleared his throat and tapped something on his side of the screen. "I found this video on my old tablet. I don't think you have a copy. It's from Ben's third birthday party. I wanted you to have it... so you can watch it when you're ready. I hope I'll talk to you soon."

The message ended, and Avia's eyes burned as the file he'd attached popped up. She jabbed at it to keep it from playing, but autoplay had already kicked on. Ben's face filled the screen. His tousled brown hair, his bright blue eyes, chubby cheeks, button nose. Avia stiffened in her seat, tears filling her eyes, but she couldn't make herself stop the video.

Ben giggled and poked at the lens. The camera panned out as Grant pulled it away, and she could see the tray of bubbles at Ben's feet. She choked back a sob and pressed her hand against her mouth. This was right before everyone had shown up for the party. She saw herself kneel down beside Ben.

"You dip the wand like this, Benny—watch." Avia's younger self, her happier self, the self who didn't know the depth of pain she'd feel so soon, passed the wand through the bubbles and lifted it into the air.

Ben smiled and helped her blow an enormous bubble. It drifted through the air, and Ben chased after it. He clapped his hands together, popping it. "More, more!"

He ran back to Avia and jumped into her lap, snuggling in close. She wrapped one arm around his chest and dipped the wand again.

Ben lifted his face to gaze up at her. "I love you, Mama."

"I love you, too, Benny." The old Avia beamed, cuddling Ben closer. "Now watch. Just like this."

The video ended there, and Avia found herself smiling, even as the screen blurred through her tears. They'd been so happy together. The perfect little family. Ben was supposed to grow up, have his own family, his own children. But all that had been ripped away from him. Too soon. The empty space inside Avia ached so badly, like bandages had been ripped off an infected wound, reminding her of what she'd never have again.

She passed her hand through the video, as if she could touch the still image of a happier Avia snuggling Ben in her lap. The image rippled in response. She saved the video to her backup drive so she could watch it again later, and as she did, the truth hit her, knocking her breath away.

Grant hadn't been able to move forward with her, because *she'd* been unable and unwilling to move forward at all.

But how could she be expected to ever move on after losing Ben? He'd grown within her womb, she'd nursed him, loved him, had gotten to know him for the short few years he'd blessed the earth with his life. No matter what, there would *always* be pain when she thought of him and what his life could have been.

But maybe... maybe the constant pain, the bitterness, the anger she felt toward Grant, toward Infinitek, toward all the things she had no power over—maybe that was holding her back. She'd lived this past year in a fog, never having the clarity she needed to move this project forward. *That* was the real reason she'd lost her funding.

New life can't grow until you make space by clearing the old.

You tilled the earth after harvest, you planted new seeds. Maybe she could have saved the Protected Project if she'd found a way to make space for it. Or was the project, like Dalton had hinted, nothing but the sad obsession of a mother who'd lost her child too soon?

Avia wiped her cheeks and pulled up her research, knowing it might be for the last time.

As she opened the list of amino acid combinations she'd been working on, her hand froze, hovering in the air. Several of them had been highlighted and were blinking. Lizzy had done something when she'd taken the holotab last night. Is this what she'd done—highlight combinations? Avia shook her head and tapped them, opening each one in turn, until they were all lined up in a row.

Something in her mind shifted; pieces moved around. And then the answer she'd been seeking crystallized in the space that opened up. She hadn't been trying the right combinations because she'd been trying each one alone. She needed to take pieces from each and assemble them to make a new combination. They went *together*.

She quickly gestured, drawing them into one file, and opened up the 3D protein model. She activated the program and waited, barely breathing, as it ran through the combinations.

Then it appeared.

100% match.

She jumped to her feet and leaned closer to the screen. Lizzy had somehow seen the solution in Avia's mind and had led her straight to it. Avia's hands shook as she commed Doctor Phan.

"You need to come to my lab right now. Infinitek's going to want to fund the Protected Project."

NOTE FROM THE AUTHOR

Note from the Author (Originally Appeared in The Telepath Chronicles)

I'm trying to be optimistic about the future, but it's not easy. You see the headlines. I'd like to believe we're addicted to sensationalism, that the newscasts show a story uglier than the truth. But they don't. And there's probably a lot more that we're not paying attention to.

I'm both fascinated and repelled by the idea of genetically engineering humans. But it's going to happen. Will we be able to prevent disease, increase intelligence, and open up new areas of the brain—allowing for real-life empaths or telepaths? And even if we can, what price will we pay? Because everything in life has a cost.

Once some of us are genetically engineered and some of us are not—will there be a new class structure? Perhaps our DNA will provide a new way to include and exclude people; perhaps it will usher in a new era where genetic prejudice is the newest ideology to cause social strife.

"Decode" is a story about the potential cost of such experimentation—but it's also a story about the hope we hold for a better future, and the belief that we can, with our resourcefulness and technology, deal with whatever happens next. I sit on the razor-thin edge between these two visions—excited about what we can achieve, but terrified of what will happen if we don't properly weigh the costs before acting.

"Decode" is an origin story for my Fractured Era series (Defective, Legacy Code, and Sun-Path). All the books in Fractured Era tell the story of the costs associated with Infinitek's experiments, including Avia's Protected Project. Everything in life has a cost... and Infinitek's projects demand a price that must be paid for centuries.

Sign up for my newsletter at AutumnKalquist.com to get free songs from the series and learn more about Fractured Era.

FRACTURED ERA
SERIES

DEFECTIVE

DEFECTIVE
INFECTED
PROTECTED

LEGACY CODE

LEGACY CODE
PARAGON

FRACTURED ERA
ARCHIVES

318
DECODE
BETTER WORLD

www.ingramcontent.com/pod-product-compliance
Lightning Source LLC
Chambersburg PA
CBHW020319150626
46552CB00022B/2985